*Friends in High Places*

These words are written for the young
– and the young at heart –
and especially for our grandchildren,
all of whom have reminded me
of important things I had forgotten.

# Friends in High Places

*words of inspiration*

Una O'Higgins O'Malley

ISBN 1–903631–49–1, *paperback*



First published in January 2005 by

Arlen House
PO Box 222
Galway
Ireland

42 Grange Abbey Road
Baldoyle
Dublin 13

arlenhouse@ireland.com
www.arlenhouse.com

Cover courtesy of Pauline Bewick
from a private collection

Typesetting: Arlen House
Printed by: ColourBooks, Baldoyle, Dublin 13

CONTENTS

# INTRODUCTION

The basis for each of the twelve stories recreated here is recorded in one or more of the Gospels, but not all the people described here are to be found in those pages. It is hoped, however, that what is written is faithful to the wonderful pictures that Jesus gave us, ie, of his loving Father, of a good neighbour, of his own special love for children. Some of the stories are about Jesus himself – he is the healer, the teacher, the minder of sheep; others are stories which he told in order to explain better what he meant. The thing to remember is that, unlike Superman and Action Man, Jesus is *real*: he actually lived in this world, bringing God's love to us all.

"The Cousins" is based on Luke Ch 1. "Wine at the Wedding", (John Ch 2, v 1-11). "Sarah's Secret", (Matthew Ch 19, v 13-15; Mark, Ch 10, v 13-16; Luke Ch 18, v 15-17). "Joe's Backpack", (John Ch 6, v 1-14; also see Matthew Ch 14, v 13-21; Mark Ch 6, v 30-44; Luke Ch 15, v 1-7). "Bobby, the Blacksheep", (Matthew Ch 18, v 10-14; Luke Ch 15, v 1-7, see also John Ch 10, v 1-18). "Naomi's New Song", (Mark Ch 5, v 21-43; Matthew Ch 9, 18-26; Luke Ch 8, v 40-56). "The Bridesmaids",(Matthew Ch 25, v 1-12). "The Hitchhiker, the Muggers and the Halfway House Inn", (Luke Ch 10, v 30-37; Matthew, Ch 22, v 34-40; Mark, Ch 12, v 28-34). "The Return of the Big Spender", (Luke Ch 15, v 11-22). "The Widow's Son", (Luke Ch 7, v 11-17). "Martha and Mary's Party", (Luke Ch 10, v 38-42). "The Rich Young Man", (Matthew Ch 19, v 16-22; Mark Ch 10, v 17-31; Luke Ch 18, v 18-30). All Bible references are from the New Revised Standard Edition (Catholic Edition).

# Friends in High Places

## Christmas Lullaby , 2003

So now we sing our songs to you, we croon to you,
Cradled on shoulder high we walk the floor with you,
Murmuring the story of your birth to you,
Reminding of tiny clothes your mother fashioned
During her visit with Elizabeth.

The shawl prepared in wonder by your gran'ma
The patient confidence of your guardian Joseph,
The youthful courage of the virgin, Mary,
Her gaze fixated on your baby beauty,
Her generous breasts stinging with milk to welcome you,
The glorious harmony of the angelic chorus,
The strong simplicity of the local herdsmen,
The strange sophistication of the magi.

We tell it again over and over to you
Recalling all the details of your coming,
Hoping, beloved infant, you will listen
And will once again spend time among your people.

# The Cousins

Mary was young, still in her teens, and she had just heard the most astonishing news the world has ever known; she was to become the mother of God. It tells us much about Mary when we think how calmly she received this message - she made no fuss - and it tells us much about God, too, because it was only after she said "YES" to his invitation to her to be his mother that his coming among us started to happen.

When the angel came to Mary and told her what God wanted she answered him much as she had dealt with everything in her life up until then. She had always trusted God, loved him, praised him, spent time with him, so that what she heard on that very special day, special for you and for me and for all people ever born, was handled by her in the same way that she had handled everything else in her life - lay it before God and if he says it is good and true then go for it.

Like all mothers expecting babies she began thinking about what would need to be done to prepare for her little one's arrival. But the angel had told her other news as well - her mother's cousin, Elizabeth, was also expecting a son! Now

Elizabeth was not young - indeed it had been said that she was way too old to have any more hope of a child - but, with this news, all her disappointment and feelings of failure would vanish. It was wonderful! Elizabeth and Mary's own mother, Anne, were first cousins and had always been great friends, and Mary thought of her cousin Elizabeth with something of the same deep affection in which she held her own mother. How could Elizabeth manage now? Wouldn't she need some help? Sadly her husband had lately suffered a stroke - at least it seemed a bit like a stroke because he wasn't able to speak - but he could move around a bit, and it was thought that with the excitement of his son's birth he just might be able to talk again.

So being the sort of unselfish person she was, Mary set out next day to visit Elizabeth and to make sure that she was alright. She brought with her the best wishes and prayers of all the family and as many presents from them as she could manage to carry! One or two of the elders wondered whether she should go alone so far, but she calmed their fears. She would be fine; what better way could she prepare for the birth of her child than to help Elizabeth first and learn from her experience? Singing happy songs to God while making her way up the hilly countryside where Elizabeth lived, Mary talked with him about many things - difficult things made simple because she had such faith in him, and simple things like the wildflowers and birdcalls surrounding her, the marvellous work of his hands.

Drawing near, at last, to Elizabeth's home Mary hoped that her coming would not take her too much by surprise. It wouldn't do to give her a shock, or Zachary, her husband either. So she knocked gently on the door of her cousin's house, to be answered at once by a loud cry of welcome from inside even before the door was opened. "Come in", called Elizabeth, "come in, my very dear one, oh come in!! What a marvellous, glorious day for us that you, the mother of our God, have come to visit us. The son within me has recognised your knocking and he has jumped for joy because you are the most blessed of all women, and you carry within you the Blessed One of all humankind".

Then, putting her arm around her, Elizabeth drew Mary in, taking her cloak from her and helping her with her baggage. So we shall leave them there together, enjoying each others' company for a few weeks, busily weaving and sewing and making clothes for their babies and preparing the way for Elizabeth's son, who would be called John, and one day would baptise Mary's son Jesus, his saviour.

## Anniversary

I prayed for them today - the unsung women
Who on that Sunday afternoon
Amid the welter of surgeons and of politicians
And family members come to say farewell
And callers at the door
And weeping guards outside
And telephone enquiries
And newspaper reporters
Maintained a modicum of normality

In that bloodstained household
And kept the kettles boiling
And fed and bathed the children.

*(in memory of 10 July 1927*
*the day of my father's death)*

# Wine at the Wedding

Matt was very pleased. The manager of the big hotel nearby had sent word that he would be wanted as extra help at an important wedding-party that was booked in at the weekend. Matt had worked at this hotel before, part-time, in their busy season and he had hopes of being taken on full-time when there was a vacancy. It was a good sign that they were looking for him now for this event, he thought. So he planned to work hard at the dinner and to look his smartest, and he would then be in the good books of the head waiter.

It turned out to be a very crowded party - all sorts of people came along to drink the health of the young couple and it was quite a job pleasing them all. Matt always enjoyed weddings because of their colour and excitement and he liked seeing people of different age-groups - from small children to their elderly grandparents - having a good time together.

One group had caught his attention just now - a young man with a number of his friends was speaking with a woman who turned out to be his mother, and she seemed worried. Matt would have liked to listen in to what they were saying but all he managed to hear was the son telling his mother that his time had not yet come (whatever that meant!).

Just then the head waiter, looking very anxious, signalled to Matt to go easy with the wine he was pouring and, before long, he understood that the supply of wine had run out completely; what the waiters were then pouring was the last of it! The head waiter and the manager looked helpless, the sun shone less brightly, the future of that hotel and the jobs of all its staff were in the balance. As for the families of the bridal couple and for the young pair themselves, it would be a horrible ending to their big day, something they might never live down. All these concerns could be read in the face of the lady talking urgently with her son. Matt thought she was beautiful - no doubt her son did also. So, when she moved smilingly towards the worried staff gathered together near the door to the kitchen, he smiled back, and when she asked them to do whatever her son directed, he nodded willingly.

"Fill up the large stone jars with water, all twenty of them", the young man said.

Straightaway Matt and his friends hurried to do just that. Nothing seemed silly about it; nobody asked, "what has water to do with it, I thought it was wine we're looking for?" There was something about this man and his mother that gave them confidence and so they ran with the water, splashing a bit here and there in their haste, but nobody minded. When the jars were full up to their very brims he said, "Now draw out some and take it to the head waiter to taste, as you always do". It fell to Matt with shaking hands to bring the goblet of red - yes, dark red - liquid to his boss for his opinion. The head waiter, pursing his lips, sniffed the offered goblet, enjoying its bouquet (he had not known about the empty jars being filled up with water, he was so busy talking to the manager about what they could do next). Expertly he rolled the sample around his mouth and finally swallowed it. With amazement he hurried to the bridegroom's side. "Sir", he said, a bit stiffly, "it is usual to offer your best wine first when the people arrive and then serve the less good later but, for some reason, you have kept back this excellent wine until now". And clapping his hands to his staff he directed them at once to get busy serving what the stone jars contained.

The lady smiled delightedly at her son and his friends. The band struck up a lively tune, the bridegroom kissed the bride and later the head waiter said to Matt: "I believe we shall be expecting extra business soon, Matthew, and I shall place your name before the manager for a permanent position because I was pleased with you today, even if I did find some wine spilt on the courtyard stones". (So even the water they had splashed had turned to wine, thought Matt!) On his way home, fingering the bridegroom's generous tip, gazing at the crescent moon and stars in a velvet sky, Matt thought about that amazing day in Cana's soon-to-be-famous hotel and of a mother and son who had won his heart.

## First Mass

They stood beneath the creaking cross
Those three concelebrants
Holding together in grief, creating a cup
Of unity in which to offer up

Their dear one.
It wasn't then a time for keening or for moaning
Only three hours for standing and for praying.

At His command they would complete their vigil -
'Ite missa est' - 'it is accomplished'.

(Strange that at the original sacrifice of Calvary
Two of the priests were women?)

# SARAH'S SECRET

Sarah was six and she had a secret - a secret so big that she wanted the whole world to know it! Her heart sang as she raced down the hill towards her home - faster than she had ever been able to run before.

Sarah was the youngest in her family and she had been a delicate baby. So she was used to being told what she could and could not do by her older brothers and sisters, as well as by her parents and her Gran. Today, for example, although it had been disappointing, it had not seemed unusual when those cross men with the teacher up on the hill had said to her and her friends, "Off with you now, you're all much too small to be bothering him". "Alright, alright", she thought, "but me and my friends weren't going to bother him. We only wanted to peep through the gaps between the big people and to see him and to know why everyone is so excited about him". Her owm parents, for instance, had Ieft things at home in a way she had seldom seen when they got word that this teacher was coming their way. It was she, small Sarah, who had had to close the latch on the gate so the sheep wouldn't escape because her father had lost the head completely and strode off with the crowd without even thinking of it! Her mother had been almost as bad, though she had thought to call out to Sarah's grandmother to keep an eye on the baking loaves before she, too, hurried off. Gran was too old and stiff to make it up the hill so she agreed to look after the bread (while muttering something about young people nowadays always being in a hurry somewhere else).

It was to Gran now that Sarah would excitedly whisper her secret; well, it wasn't exactly a secret because lots of people had seen it happen. But still it was a secret because only she knew just what the teacher had said to her, talking to her as if she was a grown-up! Only she knew how his eyes had looked when he called her by her name, when he had hugged her and blessed her and all her friends, laughing with them when, in their happiness, they had danced ring-a-rosies around him. But she knew she wouldn't quite be able to explain it all - how he had managed to have babies on his lap and toddlers on his shoulders and somehow to know the name of each and everyone of them. Perhaps she would try telling it to her pet lamb tonight before she went to bed; he seemed so wise and always agreed with her.

It was when they were being turned away disappointed that the teacher had caught sight of the children and asked that they be brought back, should come up right beside him and had said to the grown-ups that if they were not like children they wouldn't make it into heaven! How come he knew the name of each child? How come he spoke to each of them as if he had known them all their lives? To her he had said; "Sarah, sweetheart, you will grow strong now, strong and kind and brave". And she *would*, she knew she would! Because if there was love like his in the world and you had been wrapped in it you'd have to share it. Wouldn't you? All she wanted now was to hug everyone else the way she had been hugged. "Gran, darling", she said, "maybe you won't have so much pain now if I put my arms around you just after he has put his arms around me?" A small flicker of hope wakened in her gran'ma's heart. By any possible chance could this wandering teacher be the Promised One in whose coming she had always believed, the long-awaited Saviour up on their hill? Surely not! But here was her little Sarah standing sturdily before her with a strength, a courage, a grace, and a light in her eye which she had never seen before. Leah wept as she and Sarah clung to each other; how glad she was that the little one was wearing the new dress she had stayed up all night to finish not so long ago when she had had nothing nice to wear on that special visit to her cousins. "Oh, alannah", she said, "maybe he is the one I have been waiting for - and to think he has embraced and blessed you!" Then straightening up with an ease she had not felt for years, Leah turned to baking more bread. Tonight it must be shared in celebration!

## EASTER 2004

What does the blue tit know of Resurrection
As she speeds from bush to hedge in search of snacks
For her demanding nestlings?

What does the lean cat know of Rising,
Padding persistently after the one man who feeds her?

And do the cherry-trees know our Saviour
As they raise their lacy parasols of petals
In pink and delicate white surrender?

What do I know of Him that I may bid him welcome
Back from the very depth of loneliness and desolation
Into his astonishingly lovely world?

## Joe's Backpack

Joe, by the age of ten, knew that if he wanted to get anywhere in life he would have to help himself. Most of his friends were still living as many children do, taking time off from lessons whenever they could to play games, but Joe already was on the look-out for ways in which to improve his lot and that of his family. Perhaps he *was*, as the neighbours said, "old before his time, way too serious", but Joe looked at his mother, working late at night so as to make money at the local market, and at his father, out in all weather fishing in a boat of which he owned a small share, and he knew he would have to earn extra money whenever he could. Because Joe was the eldest of four children and three-year-old Ben, the youngest, wasn't yet walking - perhaps he never would. Something was wrong with his left leg and mostly his father, or mother or Joe gave him a piggy-back whenever they were going anywhere together. But what would happen as he grew bigger? Joe worried about his kid brother; if they had money they could bring him to a good doctor, or maybe the famous healer that everyone was talking about would take a look at him.

"That's it", thought Joe suddenly. The healer was going to be not far from their area tomorrow, he had heard. Joe decided to join the crowd following him, sell snacks to the people and talk to the healer about Ben. "Mum", he said, "can you give me some of your bread to sell at the rally tomorrow? And I'll get some fish from Dad tonight when he comes home as well".

So Joe set off very early next morning but the distance was further than he had thought and his legs grew weary climbing up the hilly roads in the heat of the day with the pack on his back. A huge crowd had already gathered by the time he got to the meeting-place - masses of people pushing and jostling, trying to get closer to the famous man who was said to be able to cure all sorts of diseases and sickness. Poor Joe's heart sank. All he could see was the backs of the people pressing round him; there was no way he could get anywhere near the man himself to talk to him about Ben.

Just then another latecomer arrived, or rather not an actual latecomer for it seemed he had been there earlier with the healer and had been to the village in the hope of getting some take-away food for all these people - without success. "Any luck, Andrew?" one of his friends called out from the middle of the throng when they saw him returning. Seeing Joe's little backpack of bread and fish Andrew threw his eyes to heaven! A lot of use that would be among so many. But anyway he mentioned it to his leader when he finally managed to get back to him.

"Everybody should sit down", said a quiet voice in the midst of all the babble, and strangely all those thousands of people seemed to hear it for they did just that, sat down quietly in an orderly way. "Come to me, Joe", the voice went on and Joe made his way without difficulty straight to the teacher's side - spellbound. "Please may I have your fish and your loaves", he asked, and without hesitation Joe scrabbled for them in his bag and handed them over, never thinking about the price. Then when the teacher had blessed them his friends handed them round to all that crowd and absolutely everyone was fed - all those thousands of people - from Joe's backpack. (They even took up baskets full of leftovers; Joe counted at least twelve of them). "Joe", said the healer, "thank you so very much for giving all of us our supper today and please give my special love to Benjamin".

It was very late that night when Joe finally reached his home. His legs indeed were tired but his heart was singing. Never mind that he was out-of-pocket for what he had handed over to the healer; his parents would understand and he'd make it up to them some other way, because, now that he had met this man, been thanked by him, he was fit for anything. And even though he hadn't managed to talk to him about Ben he somehow felt all would be well with him now; after all the healer had known his name, sent his special love to him. So, as he came down the road towards his home, he was not really surprised that, late and all as it was, a small figure and a wildly barking dog came racing to meet him. "I don't know exactly how it happened", said his Mum, "but just as we were saying the blessing at supper-time Ben jumped up and he hasn't sat down since. Do you think that was the time that the healer blessed our bread and fish, Joe?"

## A Dublin Dancing-Class in the 1930s

The Protestant girls wore lovely lacy stockings
their mothers knitted as they watched the class
but my bookish Mum could scarcely hold a needle
and Gran was into three-ply that would last

The Protestant girls had dainty fuzzy hug-me's
in lavender or pink or palest blue,
their shining curls seemed never to look greasy
as my limp bob was sadly wont to do.

The Protestant girls had fathers who would drive them
on Sundays to the mountains or the sea;
they worked high up in banks or in big business
- but mine was only part of history.

As you grow up the whole perspective changes
and few things matter like they used to do
but somehow I remember patterned stockings
and shining curls with smiling eyes of blue.

These things are never noted in the annals
where wars are dated each with its treaty;
only to some are they at all important
and for a time they meant a lot to me.

# BOBBY, THE BLACKSHEEP

His full name was Bobtail, but his minder called him Bobby as a petname. He had special names for them all - Bobby's family - and the others nearly all followed him wherever he led them. But although Bobby loved him too he was a bit of a lad, and he had a few pals who, like himself, liked a bit of adventure. "The Gang of Four" others called them, as they jumped ditches and managed somehow to dodge under fences placed there to contain them. Indeed the Gang of Four were the nuisance of the entire neighbourhood munching other peoples' tasty young vegetables, nibbling their delicious rosebuds and leaving messes everywhere. Angrily the neighbours would complain to the shepherd, "can't you do something to control them? My new olive grove is destroyed and I'll be sending you the bill!" The shepherd would humbly apologise and quickly mend the fencing but before long Bobby and his mates would think of something else and be off on their travels again.

One day Bobby thought how nice it would be to get to a lake he had heard about from one of the elders of the flock when he was a small lamb. But that relation had died now and the rest of the family were so silly they had no idea of anything beyond the fields in which they lived. So Bobby and the rest of the gang set off on their own, one fine day, leaving the others munching dully in their peaceful pastures.

The sky was blue and the larks sang, and soon the sun grew very hot. How nice it will be, they thought, when we get to the lake and can cool our feet in it! But it seemed very far away and one by one the others grew tired and hungry and they thought of excuses to turn back, leaving Bobby to forge on alone. He wasn't lonely, he told himself, just look at those baby rabbits playing around and then darting into their holes when they saw him! He'd show them! And he could smell the water of the lake and feel its cooler air around him now. Indeed as he came round the very next corner he saw it below him - shining, vast, wonderful. Scrambling to get to it down a narrow dangerous path he missed his footing and tumbled over the sheer side of the cliff, fortunately getting caught by a thornbush which held on to his thick woolly coat and which was growing alone out of a small crevice in the rock. Bobby's heart thumped wildly - now he really was frightened. He couldn't possibly get back up to the path from which he had fallen and he couldn't go downwards because there was nothing below him except the sheer side of the rock and the deep lake, no longer blue and shining now, but dark and menacing as the evening shadows lengthened. Poor Bobby called and called - but without much hope. Who could hear his tired small voice against the wind which was rising and whipping up waves upon the water? But still he called piteously, called to his mother, called to his minder.

Until in the gathering gloom at last he saw a cheerful light coming along the path above him and heard the wonderful voice of his minder - that voice which he had always loved, even when he had disobeyed it - calling out his name.

"Is that you, Bobby old son? Hang on there, ladeen, and I'll soon get you up".

Bobby never knew just how he did manage to get back to safety; a rope had been lowered and expert hands had somehow lasooed and rescued him.

The ride home was lovely - no scolding, no reproaches - as he lay safely there on the broad shoulders and warm neck of that master-minder of his. This had to be the very best shepherd that sheep had ever known.

## An Easter Hymn

"Oh let her be,
for she has done a lovely thing for me"
he said, when generously she brought the alabaster jar
for his anointing. And so his loneliness was eased
and her extravagance became economy.
Veronica offering a tender towel,
needing to show her deep solicitude,
Simon lending a shoulder strong when his was weak,
the blind, believing thief in shared disgrace;
whenever there is sung the Easter hymn
we celebrate them, thankful there were some
who, in their characteristic ways,
could sweeten even such an agony.

# NAOMI'S NEW SONG

Naomi's parents were desperate; their beloved little girl, their only child was dangerously ill and the doctors they had consulted could, at this stage, only shake their heads in sadness. "Look", said her mother with one last hope, "there's nothing for it now except to go to a faith-healer. My sister, Lucy, says there is one going around at present doing the most astonishing things". Her sorrowing husband looked up. What would his friends on the board of his church think if he consulted such a man? They too had heard about the healer Lucy spoke of and were not at all sure what to think of him. He was attracting more and more followers and it would surely all end in trouble. But, on the other hand, suppose he *was* from God – as some people said ...? Just then Naomi's nurse hurried in to warn that her fever was rising. That decided Jairus, her father. Hastily he left a few instructions and set off to find the famous healer.

But when at last he did manage to find him there was another problem - trying to get through the crowds of people pressing about him so as to have a word in his ear. But Naomi's father was not one to give up easily and now his whole heart was in his search so he called out again and again, "Oh come our little one is dying. Come and heal her quickly, please COME!" But the crowd kept milling around the teacher and it was so difficult to explain that there was no time to waste. And there was a woman who was delaying things further and all because she had had a bleeding for twelve years! Couldn't that wait a little longer, Jairus thought; after all she had managed for twelve years, the length of Naomi's whole lifetime and really there seems no great hurry about it now, whereas, by now Naomi might even be ...!

Even as he thought of her he was gripped with fear. Some friends in the crowd who had just arrived were shaking their heads at him, signalling to him that it was too late, that he should go home and leave this man to look after the others clamouring around him.

But quickly the teacher grasped the situation. "Look, don't be afraid; keep believing! I'll be with you in a moment", he said to Jairus, "after I have explained to this lady that it was her own faith which healed her". And strangely Naomi's dad relaxed and he knew that he too believed and that in the hands of this man all would still be well. He had such a presence, a way of dealing with people that you just knew you could trust him. How could you doubt him?

Arriving back home with him and three of his friends Jairus marvelled further; the teacher simply took over the whole scene, wasn't a bit put out when the people who had gathered mocked him for saying the child was only asleep. They should know death when they saw it, some of them shouted, because they had seen it all too often before; who was this fellow to doubt them? But before they knew it the healer and his friends had bundled them all out of the house - friends, relations, musicians, all except Jairus and his wife and Naomi's nurse and his own three companions.

Then, taking the child's cold small hand in his own big warm one, very gently, but clearly, he said, "Little one, get up". And straightway, smilingly Naomi did just that, moved about hugging her parents and her nurse while they smiled back and wiped away their tears at the same time. "Don't say a word to anyone about what has happened", said the teacher.

"Let people think what they like; what is needed now for her is food". "And for him and his friends and for us all", breathed Naomi's mother to herself as she hurried to the kitchen, remembering that in the awful expectation of a funeral a lot of extra groceries had been laid in. Now they would make a wonderfully happy feast instead. "Come in, come in", said Naomi's father hastily to the offended people outside, "come in and dine with us and, if we are lucky, Naomi will sing and dance for us because today she has learned a beautiful, new song that she has never sung before - a new song to the Lord".

## Parenting

The swans have brought their cygnets around to call
Five fluffy chirping bundles full of joy,
The swallows are teaching nestlings how to fly
From our back porch
Cleaving the air at breakneck speed with pride

In their existence.
Both sets of parents have worked hard
To make this contribution
Concentrating utterly on their task
Of building, hatching, feeding, nurturing
The next generation.

After the swallows have departed it will be a task
To clean the floor under their nursery
And will the fishing–rod ever be the same
Since they have splattered it with dung
And tiny feathers?

But how can we repay
Their dedication and the thrill
Of seeing their work
So breathtakingly accomplished?
Something of our hearts will travel south with them
Praying for their safe return next summer.

# THE BRIDESMAIDS

Rachel and Ruth were twins - not identical in appearance, and their characters were rather different - but they got on well enough together. Their interests were often quite unlike, however, and now in their teens this was becoming more clear. Take their approach to their cousin's wedding, for example. They had been invited to be two of the ten bridesmaids and the difference between their preparations was like the difference between the twins themselves. Each was pleased, excited, revelling in the prospect of the new dress, the trendy hair-do, the music, flowers, banquet and dancing. Each wondered whether she would meet there someone new, someone special! This was going to be a splendid affair in a large hotel surrounded by lovely grounds. These relations were rich.

Their aunt, the mother of the bride and a sister of their own mother, was the chief organiser on their side of the family, taking charge of so many details that the twins' heads whirled as they listened to her! But one thing Ruth did remember carefully - it would be an evening wedding and the bridal party would wend its way through the hotel gardens, lit by lanterns held by the ten bridesmaids. No other lights would be lit at that time so that the procession would be the focal point, their lamps shining in the darkness as they made their way to the reception. Ruth, whose own attention to detail was not unlike that of her capable aunt, wanted to know what sort of lamps these would be. "Torches", replied her aunt, "with coloured shades surrounding them to match each dress. Can you bring your own - and make sure they have good batteries?" "Oh, yes", said both girls. "No problem". But while Rachel worried about where to get shoes which would tone in with her dress and ribbons of precisely the same colour to plait through her hair, she forgot to check on her torch or get a fresh battery for it. At least she didn't exactly forget, but she kept putting it off. "I'll do that tomorrow", she thought, "and, anyway, Aunt or Ruth or one of the others is bound to have a spare". Ruth, on the other hand, knowing how the bridal couple was looking forward to the torch-lit procession through the grounds, double-checked her torch and its battery, making a pretty shade for it as her aunt had said.

The longed-for evening came; fingernails had been polished, hairs dressed with flowers and ribbons, extra bracelets and necklets borrowed, and the lovely dresses swished as the girls twirled around. The assembled bridesmaids inspected each other with admiration and envy. ("where did she get that heavenly perfume?"; "I wish I had earrings like those!"). But Aunt Anna, although obviously pleased with their appearance was never one to hang about and she soon took charge. "Form up now, girls, for the torch-light procession, we'll just have a short rehearsal", she ordered. With sinking hearts five of the bridesmaids forgot about the frou-frou of their silken skirts and the scent of their lovely posies. "Oh Ruth", wailed Rachel, "surely you brought a spare battery for me? Mine doesn't seem to work properly" and four other featherheads were equally flustered. "There's a shop at the corner, Aunt", said Rachel, "we'll run down there and be back in a minute". But, alas, that shop had just closed, and so had the next, and, by the time the rather bedraggled girls got back the bridal couple had been lit to their banquet by five bright torches whose brand-new batteries seemed to do duty for ten. And worse was to follow. The security-man, seeing these dishevelled young ladies without escorts banging on the door of the dining-hall refused to admit them to the party, no matter how hard they pleaded or told him who their parents were.

And sadly the music of the very group that they had been so much looking forward to hearing was so vibrant, so compelling, that somehow those inside failed to hear their calling.

## WORSHIP

Yesterday a sudden delight of birds
Came celebrating a shared excitement
In the sunlit trees nearby;
From tiny wrens and finches
To thrushes, blackbirds and a squabble
Of tree-creepers they sang, danced and chased
In vibrant rapture.

Was it a thanksgiving,
A common thank-you for the joy of living
To the heavenly Father feeding them?

# THE HITCHHIKER, THE MUGGERS AND THE HALFWAY HOUSE INN

Sam had to get to that meeting in Jericho, however he managed it; he just *had* to be there to meet those senior lawyers and discuss that important case with them. Sam was young, not long qualified, and this was his first big brief, given him as a compliment by his former master. He simply had to handle it well if he wanted to develop a practice and make his name in his profession.

The problem of transport was a worry, for Sam hadn't really got the price of a ride, but he couldn't let that stand in his way. He'd set out walking and hope to hitch a lift - maybe when he got as far as the Halfway House Inn. True there were known to be muggers on that road and he'd be better travelling in a crowd, but this case had come to him suddenly and there was no time now to hang around waiting to arrange a convoy with others. He'd go, anyway, and trust to luck.

But Sam wasn't in luck that day - at least not at first. The muggers, spotting him travelling alone with his lawyer's bag over his shoulder, made short work of him! Thankfully they didn't quite kill him, but when they had finished with him he couldn't move and could only call out feebly from the ditch where they had left him covered in blood. Probably they were very angry because he had been carrying so little money and so they beat him the more. "Help me, please help me", moaned Sam, whenever another traveller passed by on the road - but nobody seemed to hear him; not the politician planning the important speech he would give in the big city, not the priest reading his prayers devoutly as he hurried by. Before long poor Sam grew silent, dropping into unconsciousness, and only came to some time later to find a big man bending over him, salving his wounds and bandaging them with strips which he tore from the spare shirt he took from his travel-bag. Gently putting Sam up before him on his horse, this stranger, whose accent and dark skin showed him to be, of all things, a Samaritan! - a despised foreigner - brought him carefully to the Halfway House Inn and looked after him overnight, when in his pain and distress Sam groaned and twisted and called out in the darkness. In the light of the next day the patient felt a good deal better, but still could not put his feet under him. "Never mind", said his rescuer. "I have to be off myself to look after some business, but I'll make arrangements with the manager so that you are well looked after, and I'll be back myself in two days time to make sure that you are well enough to go home. And don't be worrying about the bill; I've seen to all of that. Just you get yourself better; try to eat, enjoy the house wine, which is weII spoken of, and take a good rest".

After the Samaritan had gone, Sam lay back on his pillows marvelling. This foreigner, this dark-skinned stranger, whose religion was not the true one, whose people were not even spoken to by Sam's people, had not only saved his life but had bathed him, nursed him, torn up his best shirt for him, sat up most of the night with him and now was treating him to two extra days at this hotel so he could recover his strength before making his way back to Jerusalem! Sam had heard talk of loving one's neighbour, but this Samaritan had a very high standard indeed of loving and an extra-large idea of who was his neighbour. Praying that he himself from now on would be able to copy this kind of loving, this kind of neighbourliness, for the rest of his life, Sam fell into a deep and refreshing sleep, dreaming not of muggers but of a kindly friend - no longer a stranger.

## Challenges

Poised on the little red-brick wall
surrounding the ornamental pond
in a pleasant Dublin garden,
the heron gazed in wonder at the
sparkling fountain.
Statuesque he stood in awe,
fascinated, questioning -
(could this be the Great White Bird
his parents told of?)

At length reluctantly he lifted off
flapping his elegant way
across the skyline
reflecting on his strange discovery.

Meantime, collars turned up against the autumn chill,
the young strode purposefully by
listening intently to their walkmans
or texting, or dealing with messages
on their mobile telephones;
for them it was another busy
working-day.

# The Return of the Big Spender

Jason had always wanted to see more of the world than his father's farm. Even as a young boy he had known that he didn't want to spend his whole life as a farmer but that, as soon as he could, he would get away and have a very different sort of lifestyle. Life on a farm was boring he told his elder brother, John - always going through the same old routine year after year, always having to look after animals and crops, no matter what else you would prefer to be doing.

John found Jason's views rather shocking - as the latter grew older he became so restless, so full of ideas about girls, theatres and the bright lights of cities. Where he got such ideas from, John didn't know - certainly not from him! He was intent on one thing only - the farm! Had there been a prize in his time for the Young Farmer of the Year he would have won it annually but, to tell the truth, he was a rather dull sort of chap, while young Jason was lively and good fun, even though he was an idler.

He certainly had a way of charming his father who, although he worried about the lad, found him very hard to refuse.

Constantly John would feel hurt whenever his father seemed to make a favourite of his younger son so that when, one day, Jason managed to coax their father into giving him the price of his share of the holding and let him off on his travels; John was not sorry. Now he and his father could get down to things together and not be upset by the lad's restlessness. Now he would be his father's favourite, he the faithful one staying with him at home and working even harder to make up for the loss of his brother.

But fathers are not always predictable and this one loved Jason even more because he had left home and was far away; he missed his liveliness about the place and forgot all his faults. How was the child doing - (it maddened John that his father would still refer to the young brat as "the child"). He had heard there was a famine in that country to which he had gone: "What would happen to him?" And many a time John caught his father gazing hopefully down the road, especially whenever Jason's dog barked excitedly.

Indeed all was not well with Jason. It had not taken very long to get through his money because lots of people were ready to help him spend it and now he was penniless and the famine was spreading. He had to try to earn his living some way and since the only thing he knew about was farming he hired himself to a farmer and was put in charge of the pigs. Poor Jason hated pigs, but there was nothing for it but to stay with them; at least he could get something to eat from the scraps that were given to them and that meant a lot because their owner was cheating him of his proper wages. But each day his strength was fading until at last he thought: "What am I doing here in this awful state, eating from pig-swill. While I still have enough energy I'll go back to my father, but this time I must be straight with him and not try to wheedle him into doing something unfair. I'll say 'Look, I have done things which make me unfit now to be called your son, but could you please hire me like the other farm-hands because I need the job'".

So, with that in mind, Jason managed to make the long journey back, at last coming within sight of his home. Whether or not it was the dog that alerted him his father caught sight of him and knew it was his boy, even though he was still a long way off. The father's heart turned over; "the child" was walking very slowly, seemed to have grown very thin. Running out along the road to meet him, his arms opened wide, the father called out a welcome and when he reached Jason he hugged him again and again. But Jason, remembering his promise to himself that he would never again play on his father's love, managed at last to stand back from him and to say what he had planned: "Dad, I have sinned before God and you and I'm not fit to be called your son - but, if you could just give me a job like the other ..." He got no further because his father would hear no more. "Quick, quick", he shouted, "we must have a wonderful dinner for this childeen of mine who was dead (as I thought) and is alive, was lost and now is found". So everyone in the household got busy - some looking after Jason and getting him ready for the party, some preparing the feast, others inviting the guests, sending for the musicians.

The house was all lit up, the music in full swing when late that evening, John, tired and hungry, came home from his long day's work in the fields. "What's this", he asked, "What's all the fuss about?" So they told him the good news of his brother's return, how a party was being given in celebration and how his father was waiting for him to join them. But the old envy stirred again in John and he refused to go in. Even when his father came out to plead with him he still resisted.

"Look", he said angrily to him, "I've been with you all these years, worked hard for you, never gave you any trouble, yet when was I ever offered a party for my friends?"

"Son", said his father, "that's exactly it; you have been with me all the time and you could have had anything you wanted from me".

But try as he would the father could not get John to see the beauty of what had happened.

"This, your own brother who was thought to be dead is alive, he was lost and now is found. Do you not understand?"

Sadly John did *not* understand and miserably he locked his heart against his brother and his loving father.

## A Cameo

After the murder of our Gran'pa she came to Donnybrook
to live behind a monkey-puzzle tree
and full-length white lace curtains.
Her sepia hall held portraits of three dear ones
each killed by violence; her drawing-room
had a case of little ivory elephants
sent by Aunt Kathleen, a missionary in India.

When you would crunch the gravel path
and climb the hall-door steps
Annie would smilingly unfold
the gate-legged table
and soon would carry up the tea-things
accompanied by buttered scones
fresh from the oven.

After Gran'ma had poured the tea
sitting upright in her quiet black
she'd listen to your stories
- ( you would have to speak quite loudly).
She liked to share your jokes
and smile and tell you you were wonderful
and you would go home feeling special.

Her small feet travelled lightly on the earth,
she made her sorrow-filled way with courage
and in quietness.

(My grandmother gave no evidence to identify her husband's killers though it was probable she had recognised them, and I never heard her say a word of bitterness about the assassination of my father. She was a daily communicant).

# The Widow's Son

They were talking him to his grave and, quite simply, she did not see how she could live without him. He was her only child, her one support; without him she had nothing and there was no further point in carrying on, in trying to live.

For many grey years she had dreaded this day - ever since she had first wondered if he was involved with the freedom fighters, the resistance movement. Not that she had ever asked him about that. It seemed ... wiser not to mention her suspicions; because that way they could remain only worries and not facts. He had come and gone from their home in his own time, in his own way. She didn't enquire how he earned the money he gave her weekly; she never commented when unusual things happened, unusual people called. Her own friends, few enough in number, became even fewer; she did not like to invite them often to her home in case, somehow, his secret might be discovered and she didn't delay much talking to them at the market either, because always she felt the need to protect him from the curiosity of others.

Now he was dead, dead from a so-called "punishment beating" in a laneway not far from where he had lived. The leaden sorrow of his passing was doubled for her by its violence, its stealth.

A crowd of curious onlookers gathered behind her as she walked with his battered remains to the cemetery, but she didn't look round at them. Nor did she look up either from behind her draped headscarf when the procession was stopped and a stranger spoke to her - but she *did* see his hand place the hand of her living son in hers. She looked up then into the most loving face she had ever seen and she poured blessings on him again and again for the rest of her lifetime.

## Old Maids

On Thursdays and on every second Sunday
In the afternoons when everything was tidy
They put on coats and hats and took the tram
To Dublin. The younger ones might meet a friend
At the GPO and post a letter home
Enclosing perhaps ten shillings – their weekly wages;
Others would spend time in Clarendon or Whitefriar Street
churches
Attending a Sodality Meeting and afterwards buying
'The Little Flower'
'The Messenger of the Sacred Heart' or 'The Madonna'
to be read by the kitchen fire at night when all was quiet
and the cat snoozed by the range and nobody was ringing
bells
or looking for their service.

Annie or Kathleen would be up at six or at the latest seven
And would then begin the raking out and stoking
of the range,
The cleaning of the upstairs fire and the cooking
of the breakfast.
For mornings she would wear a coloured dress
with large white
Cap and apron but in the afternoons would change to black
With smaller cap and sometimes a lacy collar.

Her days would go in polishing and dusting
In ironing and washing;
In fetching things and humouring 'the mistress'
And in caring for her family.
When no longer fit for work did she have sufficient savings
To support herself? Who then looked after her
In the way that she had minded others?
The hope must be that heavenly lamps
Shone out for her as she singly made
her way towards the light.

## Martha and Mary's Party

Martha and Mary were sisters who lived with their brother, Lazarus, in a country place not far from the big city. The air was beautifully fresh and cool there, not like in the heat of the crowded town. So when they noticed that their friend, Jesus, whom everyone was following, was looking tired and weary, they invited him to come and visit them. When he said "Yes" they were each delighted, but for slightly different reasons. Mary thought, "That's wonderful! I have so many questions I want to ask him and there are so many things I hope to hear him discuss". Martha, the elder sister, thought of all the many people who would welcome an invitation to come and meet their friend and she planned to squeeze as many as possible into a supper-party in his honour.

Then, of course, a day or two before their guest was expected, Martha got into a bit of a panic about the food! Heavens! what a crowd she had invited and Joanna, her friend who often cooked with her, was sick and couldn't come to help. Oh, she'd never be able to provide a decent supper for them all, and poor Martha grew cross with herself for inviting so many! And the crosser she grew, the harder she worked in the kitchen preparing more and more dishes.

Mary, on the other hand, knew that the only really important thing was to listen to their friend, Jesus, and to remember always what he said. So, as soon as he arrived, she left the kitchen and just sat with him and learned from him, certain that this was the most important thing that she could do just then. There really was quite enough to eat and it was not good to fuss over food if it meant neglecting the Master.

But soon Martha, red in the face from the heat of the kitchen, and hurt that her sister had now left her to cope on her own, bustled in to complain. Tired and vexed she scolded them both: "Do you not care", she asked their friend, "that my sister has left me alone to decorate these dishes so that everything will look just right for the party tonight?!" (After all, she thought, it's because of you I have invited so many and because of you everything must be as perfect as it can be).

Their friend looked lovingly on them both - one sitting so attentively with him, the other, her generous hands white with flour, so anxious for his comfort, so hospitable to their many friends. Smiling affectionately at Martha, he patted the chair beside him: "Come, sit with me too", he said, "Our time together is very precious and Mary really does have the right idea".

In the warmth of his smile Martha melted. Wiping her hands on her apron she slipped it off and sat down. Yes; in the end of the day only one thing mattered. You could be busying yourself about all sorts of things, but unless you really listened to him it was all a waste of time. What really mattered was to be with him. Everything else would work out alright; she knew it would!

(And just then she caught sight of Joanna, recovered from her illness, carrying the little bag in which she always brought her apron and her comfortable slippers, making her way quietly through the side entrance into the kitchen).

# The Rich Young Man

David was a popular lad. At school he had done very well, being not only good at studies, but a member of the religious sodality and ending up as head-prefect. Now, aged twenty, he had spent a couple of years in the family business and was about to be made a partner in it on his next birthday, taking charge of a whole new trade route into India and the Far East. The company dealt in expensive perfumes, herbal oils and face-creams, and had been founded by David's great-grandfather. Each generation since had built on the success of the previous one and David's father's hopes were high that now his own son, in turn, would expand the firm further and would marry the daughter of their chief rival and merge the two companies together.

David, it has to be said, was not only intelligent and good-looking - he was also a decent fellow and was known to take seriously the rules of his religion. Indeed so anxious was he to make sure, before he married, that he was doing all that was right that he made contact with the travelling teacher whom some said was the Holy One sent by God. Better be on the safe side and make sure he wasn't overlooking anything it was his duty to do. Finding this teacher had been a bit of a problem: he seemed forever on the move. And when it was clear where to locate him the trouble was how to get a word with him in private what with all the mob pressing around him (some of whom David thought could do with more than a few drops of his Attar of Roses or other perfumes to sweeten them!)

But any thing that he undertook should be done well, his school of business studies had taught him, so he pursued the man diligently and finally managed a word with him. "How shall I get to heaven'?" was the nub of his questioning, "Is there anything special which I should be doing'?"

"You know the commandments of God", said the teacher. "Keep them". "Oh, but I do", said David, "Indeed I have always done". At that stage the teacher gazed on the earnest young man with special affection. Here was a seeker who would add a lot to the group of followers then gathering around him. "'Why don't you sell your share in the business, give the money to the poor and, instead of selling passing luxuries, sell the oil of my love, the fragrance of my caring?"

The light that had been shining in David's eyes, the light of searching and hope, grew dim. This was, after all, only a rather dusty, down-at-heel wandering man with a group of not-very-educated followers. Why had he bothered to consult him? How could he possibly follow his wild promptings? What would his parents think, not to mention Deborah, the heiress he hoped to marry?!!

"Yes, well thank you, thank you", he said with some embarrassment as he began to move away, "I must think about that some time, some time, but right now I'm afraid I have to be on my way".

The teacher's eyes filled a little as he gazed after him retreating rapidly and a bit awkwardly down the road.

## Nationhood - A Celebration

Nationhood, I think, was first conveyed to me in colours,
In the misty blue and smoky grey of the Dail's
Dun Emer carpets;
Muted purple too might be included
And older women wearing Celtic brooches
And grey ribbed woollen stockings
Seemed to feature.
Nothing as brash as vivid green or orange
Comes to my memory,
The tone was far more mystical
And spare,
(if inevitably self-conscious).
And the sound was one of harp-strings;

The Abbey Theatre strove to explain another culture
To itself
But the hurdy-gurdies on Bray Head
Meant more to some
Than magisterial Ben Bulben

And in place of 'Irish Cottage Industries'
And 'the Cuala Press'
We have progressed to 'Kentucky Fried Chicken'
And outlets for the shirts of
Manchester United.

## PRAYER

Sometimes I wonder "What is prayer?" The Maynooth Catechism gives this answer, "Prayer is an elevation of the soul to God to adore Him, to bless His holy name, to praise His goodness and to return Him thanks for all His benefits".

Thankfully there is nothing specific about actually reciting prayers or of duration, and frequency only came into the next question, "At what particular times should we pray".

Strangely I don't seem to remember petition being mentioned, but, for some reason, I don't feel drawn to much specific petitioning - maybe because that's not how human friendships work; you are mainly delighted to be with your friend and to enjoy their company and are somewhat disinclined to spoil things by spelling out all your own problems. Friendship with God, our nearest and dearest, may be something the same.

At all events, for what it is worth, my soul seems to have a distinct preference for very brief, but, thankfully, fairly constant elevations of itself to its Creator, in adoration, in blessing, in praise and in thanksgiving. I can only hope that this is prayer.

Thanksgiving, I find, comes more frequently as part of the ageing process; one becomes more appreciative of things previously taken all too much for granted. Being able to get out of bed each morning and to stand upright, being sheltered from winter weather, are blessings to be counted more gratefully now. Praise? It's difficult not to praise the Creator for the marvels of this world especially now that TV brings so many of them into our sitting-rooms.

Blessing the Holy Name of God? - surely not in traffic-jams and in hectic supermarkets? But, yes, quite often even then because there is always the patient busdriver, the smiling checkout lady, who can somehow remind you of their maker. And then to give thanks there's always the opportunity, when the panting lorry didn't hit me after all, or when in the nick of time, I sensed that pedestrian was about to dash out in front of me, apparently bent on self-destruction. When going to meet a friend I invite the dear Lord to come too; when laying our table I mentally lay an extra place. If none of this is prayer then I can scarcely be said to pray at all but I cling to the hope that it helps to keep God alive in our world, our greatest task, our only task.

Experiences of prayer in Church for me can be variable - a weekday Mass, for example, can feel much more prayerful than a Sunday one. But that says nothing about how God sees it - about His/Her delight in that family of young children all struggling in a little late, in the lady beside me singing bravely but off-key, in the strong-voiced priest shouting it into a sensitive microphone as if he had no amplification.

"Your ways are not My ways and your thoughts are not My thoughts". My spirit will, however, soar in what to it feels like prayer when the young curate with the beautiful voice intones: "Through Him, with Him, in Him/ In the unity of the Holy Spirit/ All glory and honour is yours, Almighty Father/ For ever and ever!" and we affirm each line of it with an ascending crescendo of "Amen's".

In the West I somehow feel more prayerful when the Mass is interspersed with Irish and I like a post-communion reflection from some of our Irish poets. In Oughterard a sense of prayer will be encouraged by the beautiful colours in the Harry Clarke-type stained-glass window, by the unfailing flowers grown in the neighbouring gardens and by the Easter daffodils dancing at the lakeshore church in Glann. Trying to encourage our sense of Emmanuel - God with us, is that what prayer is? Following that idea my rather surprising Advent prayer came out this year as follows:

The little ones pedal and scoot their way
braving the uphill puddled path
to their creches and kindergartens,
accompanied by mothers pushing buggies
and their enthusiastic dogs.
A blackbird fidgets urgently in the copper hedge
as orange cotoneaster replaces summer's lavender.
Sharpen our focus now to comprehend your coming
with all the zest and confidence of childhood
into your difficult, dangerous
and largely inattentive
world.

Something about the spunky way the youngsters, seen from our early-morning windows, tackle their day sparked off in me the sudden realisation of the child Jesus, the small boy enthusing, delighting, achieving, and growing like every other child.

Not a static figure in a Christmas crib but a striving childeen like every other one; God-with-us, maybe not in pink wellington boots with cycle-helmet to match, but God-with-us just the same with an admiring mother and step-father to encourage and be proud of him.

Nowadays it seems as if the God to whom I most relate is to be found in churches only in the first instance. They are the power-houses, the restaurants (if that is not too disrespectful a word) in which spiritual energy is stored and dispensed, but it is when you leave them that their true worth is discovered, I think. (As in Corrymeela where the parting statement is "Corrymeela begins when you leave here"). In recent years my attempts to express that meeting with God in his wider creation have taken the form of lines such as:

Before the dawn I had a meeting with my Maker,
I sensed that in the quiet dark of fossil-water
the Spirit lies, and in the fleeting fragrance

of sweet blooms the scented goodness of the Godhead
can be savoured. I heard the ripples of God's music
in the underlying chords of my existence,
I touched the silken strength of God's own skin
in fruits and flowers,
I shared his sense of fun in fancy fishes,
admired the feathered patterns and designs
of sophisticated sculpture.
I danced and swayed to rhythms deep within me
and played at hide-and-seek among the bushes
of my fancies, knowing it was the Spirit
was my playmate. A baby's laugh
reechoed God's own singing
and nothing mattered since the world
was cherished.

But the rest of that piece goes on to relate my failure to sustain that realisation to any appreciable extent. Another effort in this search for my Maker I have called "Just God"; its second verse goes like this:

When someone speaks of God I like to hear,
God in the spare no-thingness of the deity, I mean,
not efforts to define, control, explain
and not the endless news of the foot-soldiers,
their tireless networkings and holy undertakings,
Just God around, within, both them and me,
God in the quiet of a smile, a tear,
God in the freedom of abstractions,
in the silent grief of elephants over a dead companion
and in the buzzing of a sultry bee.

Searching to discover and to express these feelings for me is prayer - at least I hope it is. If not it is only an ego-trip and a pretty ineffectual one at that! But God, we believe, is not just with us; God, we also believe is *in* us. What the Catechism answer didn't reach on, I think, is that prayer, as well as being an elevation of the soul to God, is also a digging down into oneself in search of what the Spirit there is saying. No two minds or souls are exactly the same and since each one is unique in the eyes of its Creator then each needs to try to understand itself out of respect and love for its Creator. And this struggle for self-understanding and self-expression is also a form of prayer, implicit prayer, I believe. Those of us who have had the great blessing of being baptised and confirmed hold that God is within us in a special way, but the search for Truth and Beauty goes on in others also, perhaps especially in creative artists whose task is to carry on the Creator's plan, whether or not they would so describe it. It seems to me a great pity that our Church has been rather fearful, or at any rate limited, in acclaiming this powerful form of prayer. In past centuries the arts were greatly supported by, and I suppose also controlled by, the Church. Today there would be little question of control but a greater acknowledgment by the Church of God's Spirit working in his world could build important bridges, I imagine.

Mentioning the building of bridges I'd like to refer to ceremonies that I attend nowadays: First Holy Communions, Confirmations, Marriages and (all too often) Funerals, occasions when a number of the congregation present may no longer be practising Catholics but are moved in a special way by what is happening at that time. It seems to me a terrible pity that no form of General Absolution may be given "because of the day that is in it", something which would allow people to receive Holy Communion. As it is I think that not a few receive anyway more than likely out of a feeling of solidarity with what is taking place. Is it preferable that they do so with no offering of absolution on this special day?

Confession, or the Sacrament of Reconciliation, is not now for me very compelling; perhaps it never was. But all the same I think that we Catholics are very fortunate to have it and probably we don't value it sufficiently. Nevertheless I find it next to impossible to define, much less enumerate, my failures, my deficiencies. I can say "God be merciful to me a sinner" over and over with a heart and a half, but what really is moving me is a sense of how far short I have fallen from what I might have been. How to explain this to someone, no matter how gentle and kind and welcoming, I do not know.

I have always found helpful poetry in prayer. "The Little Office of the Immaculate Conception" I found thrilling as a girl and the psalmists, too, knew well how to give expression to their messages and to their moods. "St. Patrick's Breastplate" was another powerful mover and shaker of my youth, but the awful poignancy of "Abide with Me" at a Northern funeral is in a place of its own together with its shades of Enniskillen and Omagh and wreaths of poppies entwined with struggling shamrocks.

"Help of the helpless, Oh abide with me", and Betty Williams coming to Dublin with the smoke of La Mon in her hair and the subsequent collapse of her women's movement for peace. "Oh Thou who changest not/Abide with me". And Cardinal O'Fiaich in a Christmas procession down the aisle of St Ann's Cathedral in Belfast, singing carols and bringing to that grey, Protestant edifice its first splash of cardinal red and a sudden sting of unexpected tears to my eyes.

Which brings me to ecumenical prayer and the particular place it has in my heart. It concentrates my mind in a special way and, of course, is at its most urgent, most vital, when offered by people in physical or spiritual distress. I think of one young Northern Protestant rocking in misery and, head in hands, groaning out his prayer, "Oh God, there's got to be another way! Show us another way!" I think of a Jewish Christian gathering at Kylemore Abbey where the Jewish rendering of "The Kaddish" and remembrances of the Holocaust sent strong vibrations through Christians present. Prayer in Corrymeela with young guitar-playing seekers after truth seated on the floor and strumming quiet chords to Taize chants, soaring prayer sung by monks in their Abbeys, devout prayer offered on his prayer-mat at regular intervals by a young Muslim driver chauffeuring us across an apparently unmarked Sudanese desert, have all brought to me greater awareness of our Creator. The valedictory prayer offered by Bill Clinton for the Irish did not sound to me Pollyannaish nor did the prayers offered by the rival candidates for the US Presidency for each other and for their families.

Maybe we Irish need to take a hard look at our shyness or our cynicism when we pronounce these things corny or insincere; certainly we have been taken in from time to time by apparently holy people, but one doesn't need to have led a blameless life before offering prayer. Sincerity is all that is called for; if it were otherwise which of us could pray?

But prayer in a group or congregation needs to be in tune with the common mood I think. I remember a quiet English Quaker encouraging silence at a Peace Conference workshop by breathing gently: "Be still and know that I am God", whereupon a large nun of charismatic persuasion responded with loud cries of "Alleluia, Alleluia".

Looking back to my youth it amazes me how much our attitude to parayer has shifted. Then prayer was definitely a private and personal thing between oneself and God, and the less it had to do with the people around one the better. Now there is a growing sense of God's people in community; go first and be reconciled with your brother and THEN offer your gift at the altar. This I welcome, exacting though it can be(!) but there is a certain difficulty in today's Masses, I find, in that there is little time for any personal reflection what between two collections (in Dublin), announcements (quite a lot in rural communities), communal singing and greetings of peace.

And, now that I'm well within the age bracket myself, could I put in a mention for more pastoral attention for the elderly who, after all, are in the vanguard of those likely to be called soon to meet their Maker? Certainly the young need an apostolate but do the elderly receive sufficient help in prayer that will sustain them not just in their infirmities but will encourage them to face their final illness and death in the best possible way?

All in all I'd like to put on record my deep gratitude to the very many people, most of them now dead, who nurtured my faith and tried to encourage me to pray. Mine has not been a story of compulsion and of terrorising about hell and purgatory. I seem only to remember the gentleness of nuns and of other teachers, the endless prayers of my grandmothers and the mother of my stepfather, the rosaries of my mother and my closest aunt and uncle, the hours spent in Donnybrook church by my grandaunts and -uncles, the constancy and fidelity of my Carmelite sister and the striking affection of her sisters in religion, the unfailing friendship of the religious of the Sacred Heart, the witness of many priests both within and no longer within the ecclesiastical ministry, the amazing priesthood of my stepfather in his final years, the expressed forgiveness by my father of his assassins as he held out to them the crucifix on his rosary beads. Together with my husband and family they and many friends and associates, (believers and unbelievers), have by their unselfish lives helped to foster whatever there is of my prayer life and I thank them.

(adapted from *The Furrow* - Feb. 2001)

Through its Theological Conferences in the 1980s *The Furrow* managed to make a lay woman like myself feel part of its family - something I deeply value. But the truth is that I have never been good at prayer; my fidgety mind seems less and less capable of holding itself in place for sufficient length of time to take part in real prayer, solid prayer.

## Growing Up

I would come blinking to the daylit street
knowing once more that good would always triumph;
Snow White would wed her single-hearted prince,
Shirley, Judy, Deanna would dance and sing,
Elizabeth and Margaret Rose
would wave from their London palace.
Though my own story had begun
in death and desolation
a screen of kindliness would shelter me
and my more real God
was in his heaven.

## Confirmation 4 May 2004

Glowing with love and joy and happiness
our snowdrop has become our waxen candle
lighting the lives of all around her,
sharing the Spirit with her family and friends -
- THANK YOU, our glowing hope for the future.